# The Rabbit Who Didn't Want to Go to Sleep

Lilian Edvall
Pictures by Sara Gimbergsson

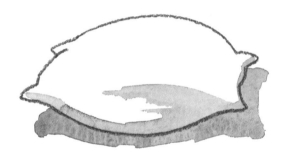

Translated by
Elisabeth Kallick Dyssegaard

The rabbit was tired, but not VERY tired.

He had watched TV.

He had eaten dinner.

He had taken a bath with his little sister.

Finally he had gotten out all his cars.
There was the Volvo and the Saab, the delivery van and the race car,
the space car and the truck, the ambulance and the police car, the
Jeep and the tired old tractor. He had made an extra-cool track for
them. He was just about to start driving the Volvo.

Then a voice came from the hall. It was Mommy's.
It said, "It's time to hop into bed."

It can't be true, thought Rabbit. I've just started playing.
"Time to put on your pajamas and choose a book,"
the mommy voice continued.

But not NOW, Rabbit thought. Not RIGHT now. The Volvo hadn't
gotten to drive around the track even once, and there was a line of
other cars that also wanted to take a turn, that HAD TO take a turn.

Rabbit took the Volvo. The engine purred. Toward the kitchen . . .
There he saw a pair of familiar paws in front of the sink.

They were Daddy's. In a friendly voice and without turning his head, Daddy said, "It's time to go to bed. Shall we keep reading the book we began yesterday?"

"Can't I stay up a little longer?" the rabbit asked while the Volvo
skidded around Daddy's leg.
"Five minutes, then." Daddy nodded and moved his paw.

The Volvo purred loudly. It drove quickly out of the kitchen. VROOM, VROOM, VROOM. Then it was the Saab's turn. Then the delivery van's. Then the race car's—that was the one that was always so impatient.

Right in mid-curve stood Mommy,
blocking the way.
"A little longer," begged the rabbit.
"A little, tiny bit longer."
"One more lap for the race car,"
said Mommy, and her voice sounded kind of tired.
The rabbit took the race car. He drove one lap,
then another . . .

He drove seven laps, he drove eighteen, he drove thirty-eight laps. He had forgotten just how much fun it was to play with the race car. Suddenly he bumped into Mommy again. The rabbit had to brake hard, and the car's tires screeched. "Just one more time," begged the rabbit, looking up.

Mommy's ears were long, but even so, they weren't hearing anything right now.

"It's late, your little sister is sleeping already, you have to go to day care tomorrow, and you have to brush your teeth."

"But I'm not done playing," explained the rabbit.

The race car tugged—it wanted to get away. It quickly changed direction. The rabbit could barely keep up. In the rush, he saw his bed. It looked still and sad, very sad in fact. He didn't want to lie there anytime soon. Onward, onward to the next room . . .

. . . where his little sister was sleeping. At that moment, the race car lost control and crashed into the nightstand. The car rolled around a few times, the trunk flew open, and something fell on the floor. The rabbit had to go get the tow truck quickly. Then his little sister woke up.

Daddy came running into the room. His front paws were wet and he looked irritated. Little sister sat up in bed, wide-awake. She thought it was morning, and wanted to have oatmeal right away.

The rabbit was in a hurry. Where was the tow truck? He didn't dare ask Mommy or Daddy. His little sister would probably help him look if she could have her oatmeal. Someone had picked up all the toys.

How was he supposed to find the tow truck now? He was forced to
dump out the box again so he could search more easily. Just then
he heard determined steps behind him. He looked around quickly.
He had to hide. Under the couch!

"This is no longer fun," said Daddy, and growled.
"There will be no story unless you come out right now,"
said Mommy, and sat down with a big sigh on the couch.
"Come o-u-t!" they called in the saddest way. But the
rabbit didn't make a peep.

He lay behind the couch. It was warm and dark there.
Suddenly he felt sleepy. Far away he heard his little sister get
her oatmeal. Soon he was snoring.

"Aha," said Daddy, who heard the snore first. "There you are."

Mommy carefully carried the rabbit to his bed. She stroked
his soft cheek and whispered, "So you were tired after all."

"But I'm not one bit tired," said little sister to Mommy.
"I can stay awake all night!"

Rabén & Sjögren Bokförlag, Stockholm
www.raben.se

Translation copyright © 2004 by Rabén & Sjögren Bokförlag
All rights reserved
Originally published in Sweden by Rabén & Sjögren under the title
KANINEN SOM INTE VILLE SOVA
Text copyright © 2003 by Lilian Edvall
Pictures copyright © 2003 by Sara Gimbergsson
Library of Congress Control Number: 2003109603
Printed in Italy
First American edition, 2004
ISBN 91-29-66001-7

Rabén & Sjögren Bokförlag is part of
P. A. Norstedt & Söner Publishing Group, established in 1823